by

Leigh Anne Florence

Illustrations by James Asher

International Standard Book Number 0-9741417-3-9
Library of Congress Card Catalog Number 2006920800

Cover design and book layout by Asher Graphics
Illustrations by James Asher

Manufactured in the United States of America

All book order correspondence should be addressed to:

HotDiggetyDog Press
P.O. 747
Shepherdsville, KY 40165

502-376-5966
leighanne@thewoodybooks.com
www.thewoodybooks.com

Dedication

This book is dedicated to all of the citizens of Kentucky.
You are what make this state so great! Enjoy the TAILS...

Foreward

A few years ago the Kentuucky Press Association's "Rockin' Readin' Revolution" statewide literacy project was just an idea in my head. Now it's an annual and sometimes semi-annual event.

Here's how it works: Kentucky newspapers publish serial stories for students and teachers, kids and families to read in their local newspapers.

In the fall of 2005, 84 Kentucky newspapers, all at the same time, published *Tails from the Bluegrass*, one chapter a week, for 10 weeks. Each week 935,000 copies of each chapter were read all over Kentucky. And thanks to Louisville Gas & Electric/Kentucky Utilities a special scrapbook was given to students to collect each chapter. The KPA website (www.kypress.com) and teachers loved them.

Tails from the Bluegrass generated so much excitement among Kentucky newspapers and their readers that Woody and his mom decided to make the story into a book — the book you're holding right now! So, as Woody would say: You, too, can take your ideas and dream like a Big Dog.

Special thanks to the Kentucky Press Association, Louisville Gas & Elecrric/Kentucky Utilities, Kentucky

Department of Education, Mrs. Glenna Fletcher, the Lexington Herald-Leader and Leigh Anne Florence for making this idea a reality.

Kriss Johnson
KPA President Elect and
Educational & Community Outreach Manager
Lexington Herald-Leader

Woody would like to thank...

Mommy and Daddy for being great parents. Dad, you are the best bus driver without a doubt. Mom, nobody can make sugar cookies like you! Doglicious! Thanks for rescuing me and giving me a home. I love you both!

James Asher - the best illustrator in the whole wide world. (By the way, Chloe and I are getting better at coloring between the line!)

The great ladies at McClanahan Publishing — Paula, Michelle, and Jo. You sure know how to put a book together.

The WOODY TEAM - Lori, Sue, Nathan, Shaun and Amanda! How could I get anything accomplished without you? Who would make my schedule? Who would help me with computer problems? Who would drive me to the post office? I don't know either.

Our new friends at Kentucky Press — David, Kriss, Bekki, Jennifer, Kevin, and Roma. Thanks for giving a wiener dog the opportunity to try his paw at newspaper writing! (Extra kisses to Mr. David from Chloe. We know she is your favorite, but NO she CANNOT live with you!)

Uncle Guy for his proofreading and literary skills.

Louisville Gas & Electric/Kentucky Utilities — especially Mr. Cliff and Mr. Chris; Mr. Gene Wilhoit and the Kentucky Department of Education; and Kentucky First Lady Glenna Fletcher (say "Arff" to Abby!).

Carla Hunter and her daughters for saying, "Hey have you ever heard of *Woody, The Kentucky Wiener*?" to Kentucky Press.

The 84 Kentucky newspapers and all the schools who participated in the "Tails" series. Hope you enjoy making the journey again!

And finally, to my beautiful Chloe. You are my sister and my business partner, but you are also my best friend. Thanks for being the greatest sister any wiener dog could ask for. I love you! Arff!

Chapter 1

Hip, Hip Hooray! Hip, Hip Hooray! I can't believe it! I've called Scruffy, Rudy, Olive, Otis, and all my friends to tell them the exciting news! Who would have known that I – Woody – an ordinary, small-town, wiener dog would be writing a newspaper column? I mean, it was just yesterday that I was using newspapers for, well, never mind...

Boy has my life changed. I've had some pretty exciting things happen in my short life! I remember the day it all started - the day I met my Mommy. Even though I was only a baby – a mere five weeks old – I remember it well. You see, a black-and-tan miniature dachshund, I was the runt of the litter – (that's dog language for the smallest of the bunch, or the underdog)! The owner of that Paducah, Kentucky tobacco farm said I would never amount to anything. When I heard this, it hurt my feelings, but I didn't let it get me down. I was determined to prove him wrong! One day this lady and her one-year old redheaded miniature dachshund came to see me. The lady bent down and scooped me up in her arms and we both instantly fell in love. I will never forget how oh-so-good Mommy smelled. Not oh-so-good like beef jerky, or rib bones, or even rawhide, but oh-so-good like fresh baked sugar cookies – my favorite, by the way! The best part – Mommy never put me down. She and her other wiener dog (Chloe, who is now my beautiful redheaded sister) took me outside, gave me a name, and the rest, as they say, is history!

"Why the name Woody?" you ask. Well, my full name is Dogwood - Dogwood since the trees were blooming when Mommy and Chloe rescued me. Everybody has always called me Woody. Well, sometimes I hear "Dogwood", like the other night when I accidentally pulled all of the garbage out of the can in the kitchen looking for one last chicken leg I thought I smelled - or when I was trying to help Chloe by eating my dinner and her dinner too. Those are the times I hear "Dogwood". When I hear "Dogwood", I know it's not going to be good!

I thought life with Mommy and Chloe couldn't get any better. I was wrong. One day Mommy came home and told Chloe and me that she had something important to tell us. I thought she was going to tell us that Scooby Doo was coming to town, or that I got a call to play ball for the Wildcats. It was even more exciting than that! She told us that she was getting married! "Married, as in, we are getting a Daddy?" That's right – married. I couldn't wait to meet our new daddy. I wondered if he was going to be wiener dog like Chloe and me, or a collie or a boxer. Imagine my surprise when Chloe explained to me that our Daddy was not going to be a pup, but a human. "A human?" Well all I can say is that he better love Mommy, animals, and the Kentucky Wildcats! As we would soon find out, Mom made a great choice!

A marriage meant twice as much fun and love, but it also brought changes - like moving from Western Kentucky to Shepherdsville, KY, a town south of Louisville that we now call home. We have a great big hill, a lake, and lots of land! We also have two brothers (Rio, a Labrador and Little Bit, a cat) and two sisters (Cheyenne, another Labrador and Dolly, another cat). As you can imagine, there is never a dull moment at our house. Someone is always barking, meowing, chasing,

SHEPHERDSVILLE
WIENER

fetching, you get the picture. Life is not all about chasing balls and kitty cats however. There is work to do. Everyone has to pitch in and do their share. Daddy calls that teamwork!

While our siblings play Watch Dog, Mommy, Daddy, Chloe, and I travel around the great state of Kentucky – and a great state it is! We have champion horses, the Kentucky Derby, Mammoth Cave, and great Bar-B-Que right here in Kentucky. We share my books in the Woody, The Kentucky Wiener series and talk to school kids about being a winner. I mean, if an ordinary, wiener dog can grow up to do great things, then so can my fellow Kentuckians! In fact, Mommy, Daddy, and Chloe are waiting in The Woody Bus as we are leaving for yet another Woody Tour! I've got my toothbrush, my monkey, and of course my map of the greatest of all fifty states, Kentucky! They are calling me so I better run, but this is only the beginning of our journey across the Bluegrass together. So get ready - this little hotdog is coming to your town! Tune back in next week to see where our Doghouse on Wheels has stopped and what we've seen and learned. In the meantime, listen to your parents, keep reading, and WORK AND DREAM LIKE A BIG DOG!

Chapter 2

Hello, Woody Readers! Here I am on my first stop of The Woody Tour. I feel like a rock star saying that. I imagine I have my own band where I play guitar and sing and Chloe is my back-up singer. We open every show with WHO LET THE DOGS OUT and the crowd goes wild! Then we stand outside our Doghouse Dressing Room while our fans hound us for PAWgraphs! Okay, back to dog earth!

I could tell you where The Woody Bus has stopped, but isn't it more fun if you guess? Chloe and I love games, so here are some clues. Are you ready?

This city was founded in 1827 by William Clark of Lewis and Clark. It is located where two rivers come together – the Ohio and Tennessee. Known as Quilt City, USA, people from all over the world come here to look at all of the beautiful, handmade quilts.

One more clue: several well-known people come from this city such as Irvin Cobb (an author from the early 1900's who wrote over 60 books), Stephen Curtis Chapman (a Christian singer who has sold millions of records, and won many Grammy and Dove Awards), and sniff, sniff, me – Woody - a wiener dog who is now on tour! That's right. We are here in my birthplace of Paducah, Kentucky. It's great to be home!

We left our doghouse in Shepherdsville yesterday morning. We crawled in The Woody Bus, buckled our seatbelts, tuned into a good radio station, and checked the mileage. 42,000 miles.

PADUCAH

We were ready to begin our journey. Since I'm from Paducah, and that's where Granny and Cousins Caroline and Patrick live, there was no need for a map. I knew exactly where we were going. I could drive, well, walk, that trip with my eyes closed. First we traveled Interstate 65 going south. Then we merged on the Western KY Parkway going, well, west. That is a long highway. Chloe and I looked at all the signs we saw along the way: White Mills, Leitchfield, Caneyville, Hartford... Wait! Why aren't there towns named after animals or dogs? Where is the town of Clifford, Lassie, or Snoopy??? Hey, we just saw Beaver Dam. That's more like it.

"WHOA! STOP THE WOODY BUS!!! What did that sign just say, Dad? It had a horse with the word 'Spirit' on it." Daddy said it was "Kentucky Unbridled Spirit." I asked him what "Unbridled Spirit" was and where Chloe and I could get some. He said Unbridled Spirit was how Kentuckians feel about their state. Kentucky is the best state in the whole US and people who live in Kentucky have great opportunities in life. He said we couldn't buy Unbridled Spirit, but we could have the Spirit by being a proud Kentuckian, learning about our state, and telling others how great Kentucky really is.

Chloe and I were talking about the people who definitely had Unbridled Spirit – Loretta Lynn, Jockey Pat Day, and the late Historian Thomas Clark, when we finally saw the sign that said, "Paducah, Next 5 Exits". We clapped our paws and jumped for joy. No more "Are we there yet? Are we there yet?" We were finally here!

Our first stop was Granny's house for a bowl of dumplings. Then we all went to one of my favorite places in Paducah - Noble Park. Before playing, we wanted to see the statue of Chief Paduke. We could spend hours swinging, sliding, and feeding the ducks. Where did all the ducks come from? Chloe and I ran out of bread. We tried to share our dog food, but Daddy said ducks don't eat dog vittles. We saw the most beautiful pictures all along the floodwall of the Ohio River. Mommy said the pictures were called murals. They were so colorful. I couldn't find any wiener dogs in the pictures. Who painted those murals by the way? We were so excited about the murals that we almost missed the Delta Queen sitting in the Ohio River. Chloe and I wondered if there were actual pirates on that boat. There could be lots of pirates in Kentucky since our state has more miles of running water than any other state except Alaska. Chloe and I can't imagine dog paddling over that much water!!! (I read that on www.travel.ky.gov/facts.)

The food, murals, and a visit to the Quilt Museum were so interesting, and exhausting. So here I am, back at Granny's ready for bed. Mommy stopped by the McCracken County Library and checked out Jesse Stuart's A Penny's Worth of Character. We love his books. He was a Kentucky author, you know? In fact, many great authors are from Kentucky such as Mr. Stuart, Wendell Berry, and Bobbie Ann Mason, just to name a few. Chloe and I have our jammies on and Mommy is ready to read. I know we have lots of sights to see over the next few weeks, but how could it get any better than Paducah? In fact, I decided this town might just be the best place in Kentucky. We'll see…

In the meantime, Work and Dream Like a BIG DOG!

Chapter 3

Chloe and I hardly slept a wink thinking of all the great things we would see in the Bluegrass State! We wondered where Daddy (the official bus driver) would take us next. Would he take us to Abraham Lincoln's birthplace in Hodgenville? Would we go to Mammoth Cave, the longest recorded cave system in the entire world? Or would we travel to Ft. Knox and try to see the country's gold reserves? Wherever we were going, we were ready!

We said goodbye to Granny and our cousins and left Paducah about 6:15 in the morning. Dad didn't tell me where we were going today but said we were going to have fun. We headed west on Highway 60 to see some sights. We hadn't been in the Woody Bus long when we decided to sniff around. Chloe and I saw the funniest sign ever: "Welcome to Monkey's Eyebrow!" We laughed and laughed and then went to find out how this town got its name. Our first stop was the General Store. Several men were drinking coffee when Chloe and I arrived. They explained nobody knew how the town got its name, but years ago people thought if you stood on a hill and looked down, the town looked like a monkey's eyebrow. I decided to put it to the test. Chloe and I climbed the tallest hill and I took out my monkey to compare. I don't know if I saw the resemblance, but it made for a great story.

After solving that mystery, back to the bus we went. While traveling along, looking at the sights and singing songs, we

MONKEYS
EYEBROW
Welcome to
MONKEYS
EYEBROW
KENTUCKY
WIENER
Kentucky

smelled the worst smell ever! "PuuuuWeeee! What is that?" I was trying to be polite, but I was sure somebody in the bus must have had an accident!!! It stunk! Mommy explained we were in Wickliffe and nobody had an accident. Wickliffe is the home to a paper factory, and something used to make paper has a terrible odor. We covered our noses and went to the Wickliffe Burial Mounds. We saw where Native Americans had ceremonies and buried their loved ones. I wondered if they knew Chief Paduke. As a pup, I didn't understand everything about the Mounds. I just know that Chloe and I were two respectful "scaredy cats!"

Monkeys Eyebrow, stinky paper, gravesites… This hot dog needed lunch. At that point we saw "Welcome to Bardwell!" "Hi, Bardwell! Do you have a place where two hot dogs can grab lunch?" Daddy pulled into HUCK'S STORE. He fueled up while Mommy, Chloe, and I went for food. We loved the store. It had candy and ice cream and cookies – all the things dogs can't eat! Mommy said since we had been good that we could pick out one treat. Chloe and I decided to share a Moon PieÒ. I wasn't sure what a Moon Pie® was, but it looked tasty! We were paying for the Moon Pie, gas, and a copy of The Carlisle County News, when I spotted the scariest thing ever! It was scarier than a snake, a vacuum cleaner, and even the Burial Grounds. At the counter, they were selling HOT DOGS!!! All of these hot dog wieners were rolling around being cooked! Chloe and I let Mommy pay while we bolted out of HUCKS! Daddy started the bus, Mommy jumped in, and we trucked on down the road!

We drove 12 miles before stopping again - just enough time to for us to finish our doglicious Moon Pie! We had arrived at our final destination – Columbus! Chloe and I couldn't wait to go to Columbus Belmont Park. Chloe and I love that Kentucky has so many beautiful state parks. In fact, Columbus

Belmont is one of forty-nine state parks in Kentucky! We had so much fun swinging and sliding down the slides. While we were resting, Daddy told us how Columbus was almost the capital of the United States. After Washington D.C. burned during the War of 1812, engineers said Columbus was the geographic center of the United States. They developed this land thinking it would be the capital, and named it Columbus, after Christopher Columbus. It wasn't chosen the capital, but the name remained!

Columbus may not have been the capital, but it still had a fantastic park. Mommy pulled out A Penny's Worth of Character and continued with the story of Shan. What a great book! I think Shan is going to get in trouble, like when Daddy calls me "Dogwood!" I think he is going to steal something from a store. He should pay before running out, even if they have hot dogs at the counter.

We had decisions to make. Since we were at the western tip of Kentucky, should we turn east and go back through Kentucky, or should we go further west into Missouri, north to Illinois, or south to Tennessee. We took a vote and crawled back into the Woody Bus! We were on our way…

WORK and DREAM LIKE A BIG DOG!

Chapter 4

Hello, Woody Readers! After a week in Western Kentucky, it was decision time. Since we were in Columbus, Kentucky, we could head west into Missouri, north to Illinois, south to Tennessee, or turn back east to enjoy more travels in Kentucky. Easy decision! Hard decisions are things like, "Do I have bacon or chicken? Do I play with my monkey or my rubber ball?" Kentucky won unanimously! Besides, our Unbridled Spirit was growing as we had learned so many great things about our state. We wanted to see how big the spirit could get! We also wanted to find the very best place in Kentucky! What better way than to keep traveling the Bluegrass! We unfolded the Kentucky map of 120 counties.

We saw some unique names like "Fancy Farm" (whoever heard of a farm that's fancy?), "Coldwater" (I prefer hot bath water.), and "Possum Trot", (what can I say?). Bowling Green caught Chloe's eye. "If we can't play ball for the Cats", Chloe said, "Maybe we could try our paws at bowling." She is so smart! Bowling Green it was.

Mommy said "Great choice!" She had a surprise for us. We couldn't wait! Mommy told us we would see in about 55 miles. We checked the mileage – 42,242. Then we did our usual, "Are we there yet?" routine. Mommy made us count the miles (with 8 paws between us, it was easy) and we finally arrived.

"Welcome to Murray State University!" We were at the place Mommy went to college. She and Daddy took us on a campus tour. It looked so exciting. Chloe and I wished we could go to college. She told us wiener dogs didn't go to college, but promised we could visit another university soon. We had to say "Arff" to Murray, but not before stopping at Sammon's Bakery for a burger and the newsstand to buy a copy of The Murray Ledger & Times. As doglicious as those burgers were, it made me wonder why anybody would ever want to eat a hot dog!

We took our time traveling from Murray to Bowling Green. We went over Kentucky's two largest bodies of water and through many towns before arriving in Bowling Green. The first sign we saw said, "Greenwood Mall". "Hey! Shouldn't that be GreenWOODY Mall?" Since Mommy had shown us where she graduated, Daddy had to show us his Alma Mater. "Western Kentucky University – Home of the Hilltoppers". It was time to stretch our legs and tour the campus. There were so many buildings, people, trees, birds, and squirrels. It was a dog's paradise. Everything was going great until Chloe started barking. She had spotted a big red monster! It wasn't Clifford and she knew things were going to get ugly. She barked and growled before Daddy picked her up and said everything was going to be fine. Then, he invited the big red monster to join us. When Daddy said he wanted to introduce us, we thought he had lost his marbles. It wasn't a monster after all. It was BIG RED, the mascot of the WKU Hilltoppers. Big Red shook our paws. We found out he knew the Wildcat of the Kentucky team, the Cardinal of the University of Louisville, and was a Clifford fan himself. He was our new friend.

We told Big Red about our tour. He wanted to show us around. Red took us to the National Corvette Museum. We couldn't believe our eyes. We saw the coolest cars! Chloe and

BOWLING GREEN
WKU

I wanted a Corvette. Mommy said Corvettes were expensive and wiener dogs didn't drive. Big Red wanted to treat us to a ride in a Corvette. We clapped and barked! There was one problem. Corvettes are sports cars and sports cars are small. Plus, there were four of us and a big red mascot. The car only held two people. Chloe decided I should be the one to ride in the Corvette with Red. She is the best big sister! Wait ! Can a mascot drive? Red indicated it was safe. Mommy said to buckle my seatbelt, mind my manners, and be back at 4:30. I had thirty minutes.

Red took me to the Fruit of the LoomÒ factory, where they once made, well, underwear. I snickered. Dogs don't wear underwear! We then traveled down Duncan Hines Highway. The man who made all those yummy treats was from Bowling Green. We went to Beech Bend Park and the Warren County Library. We were having a great time – until I checked my Scooby watch. OH NO!!! It was 5:15 and I was late! "Red, we have to go now!" I knew I was going to be in the doghouse. Was this the end of the tour???

Work and Dream Like a Big Dog!

Chapter 5

Hi, Woody Readers! It's Chloe. Woody wanted me to tell you he won't be writing you this week because he is in the doghouse. Remember last time when Mommy told Woody to be at the bus at 4:30 and Woody stayed with Big Red until 5:25? When Woody returned, Mommy, Daddy, and I all hugged and kissed him and told him we were thankful he was okay. The hugs lasted about 3 seconds before my parents told Woody he was grounded. Daddy said, "Dogwood, you didn't follow the rules. We love you but you are going to be punished." Woody said he was sorry and he even cried a little. (Don't tell him I told you.) Daddy told him that he couldn't leave the bus for two days (except to, you know), he couldn't write for at least one week, and he must go to bed without dessert. (That was disappointing since Mommy had made sugar cookies.) So I decided to help Woody! He wanted me to tell you he was sorry he got in trouble and to make sure you listen to your parents and follow their rules.

Mommy said I could choose where we went from Bowling Green. I opened the map and the name caught my eye. Could it be? I had just found the town that I had to visit!!! You'll find out in a minute, so keep reading!

It was a pretty drive with all of the leaves changing. We saw a Tulip Poplar Tree, our state's tree, snuggled in the beautiful

PIKEVILLE
Jasher

hills. Though Woody was being punished, he could still enjoy looking out the window. In addition to that, we saw Kentucky's wild animal – the grey squirrel. We barked to say hello! Every time we see something great about our state, we feel proud, and our Unbridled Spirit grows!

Our first stop was Corbin to pay respect to Colonel Sanders of KFC. His chicken is "paw-licking good", as is his life's story. He had hard times but never lost determination. In fact, Colonel Sanders was in his 60's when he started KFC! Just goes to show you we can't give up on our dreams! My brother doesn't give up either. "Chloe, since I can't leave the bus, will you find her for me?" "Whom?" I asked. "Daisy Duke. She lives in Hazard!" Mommy tried to explain that the Dukes of Hazard were not in Hazard, KY and therefore, Daisy Duke didn't live here, but Woody wouldn't listen. Being the older sister, I went to the Perry County Chamber of Commerce. They verified what Mommy said. That satisfied Woody and we bid farewell to Hazard and the Dukes!

Next stop – Pikeville. Mommy told us about the Hatfield and McCoys. Thirteen people and a pig were killed as a result of that feud. Talk about a dog fight! Daddy said people in Pikeville love Pepsi. (Say that five times.) In fact, Pikeville holds a record for how much Pepsi they drink each year.

We couldn't wait to get to Pikeville College. We wanted to see if there were really 99 steps to the college. It was a shame Woody couldn't help count, but Daddy parked the bus where he could see. Mommy, Daddy, and I climbed the steps. Actually, I only climbed 37. I was dog tired so Daddy carried me the remaining 62. There were definitely 99 steps to the college!

After a short ride, saw the neatest town called "Chloe". Mommy took my picture beside the sign. Woody was happy for me, though I think he was disappointed we hadn't found

Woody, Kentucky!

We returned to the bus and headed to the final destination of the day. While driving, Mommy continued Jesse Stuart's A Penny's Worth of Character. If you have been reading along, you know it is about a boy named Shan. Everyday Shan's mother gives him paper sacks to take to the store. The storekeeper, Mr. Conley, gives Shan a penny per sack. Shan took a sack that had a hole. He knew it had a hole, but he wanted money to buy soda and chocolate. When Mommy stopped reading, Mr. Conley had given Shan the money he didn't deserve for the damaged sack. We couldn't wait to see how Shan reacted. Woody and I were hoping he would tell Mr. Conley the truth. We had almost gotten to the good part when we saw the sign: "Welcome to Clifford!" We clapped our paws! I was sure Clifford didn't live here, but I could dream. Just like Scooby was Woody's hero, Clifford was mine. I took a picture to send it to my big red friend. I knew he would laugh! It had been a great day, but we were tired and hungry. I asked Mommy whether I would write the next column, or whether Woody would be out of the doghouse. She had not decided, but was proud of how mature Woody had taken his punishment. So, stay tuned, stay safe, and in the words of my brother, "Work and Dream Like a Big Dog!"

Chapter 6

"The sun shines bright on My Old Kentucky Home..."

Boy is it great to be out of the doghouse! After being punished, I learned my lesson. In addition to staying in the bus, Daddy told me I had to learn the six different regions of Kentucky, write Chloe a thank-you note for bailing me out, and learn the words to our state song, My Old Kentucky Home. It has become a favorite! Chloe and I love singing it while driving down the road. "Weep no more, my lady, Oh! Weep no more today..." Stephen Foster wrote that song while visiting Federal Hill (now known as My Old Kentucky Home) in Bardstown. Though it was written in 1850, it didn't become our state song until 1928. For over 75 years we have been singing My Old Kentucky Home at great events such as the Kentucky Derby!

Being in the doghouse also meant "Goodbye Game Dog, Hello books!" I learned many interesting facts while reading. For instance, did you know two ladies from Louisville wrote "Happy Birthday" in 1893? I bet you didn't know the first school in Kentucky was started in Harrodsburg in 1776. The teacher, Mrs. Coomes, didn't have any books and the students didn't have any paper or pencils. They were determined that wouldn't stop them from learning. They used boards for

CLIFFORD

paper and the intestines of oxen for ink! YUCK!!! It made me realize again that we can never give up, even when things seem impossible!

Speaking of teachers, Mary Wilson, a teacher from Henderson was so inspired by her mother that she developed Mother's Day. It became a national holiday in 1916 and we have been honoring mothers since! When I read that, it made me sad I had disobeyed Mommy. I immediately apologized to Mom for not showing up at the bus on time and promised her it wouldn't happen again. She forgave me. She also explained that when we don't follow the rules, it affects lots of people. Not only did I get in trouble, but my family worried, and Chloe had to pitch in and write. Mommy squeezed me tight and told me she loved me. She reassured me I was a good dog. "Lots of people make mistakes, Woody. We just have to learn from mistakes and strive to always do our best!" I kissed her. I knew why Mrs. Wilson wanted to celebrate mothers by setting aside a day in May. I decided to honor my mother every day, not just one day a year!

I wasn't the only Kentuckian who learned from mistakes. Jesse Stuart knew about hard times. Born in 1907 in Greenup County he loved school, but had to stay home most days to help his father with chores. He finally dropped out of school to concentrate on helping his father milk cows and chop wood. At fifteen, he returned to school. After working at a circus he went to college, became a principal, and, when he was 24 years old (a pup) he became the youngest school superintendent in Kentucky! He proved that a country boy from Kentucky could accomplish great things by working hard! Talk about Unbridled Spirit!

That inspired me. I wanted to read more success stories, so I went to www.kentuckytourism.com and found a list of people from small towns in Kentucky who had done great things. I felt silly for thinking I had to be from a rich family or live somewhere like Chicago to make a difference. My parents are always telling Chloe and me to set goals, dream big, and work hard. I was going to work and dream like a big dog and encourage others to do the same!

Speaking of doing our best, you're probably wondering what happened to Shan in A Penny's Worth of Character. When Mommy stopped reading, Mr. Conley had given Shan money he didn't deserve. Shan had tricked the store owner by taking money for a damaged sack so he could buy a chocolate and soda. When Shan returned home, his Mother was waiting for him like Mommy had waited for me a few days ago. She told Shan she was disappointed in him for letting Mr. Conley pay him for a damaged sack. Shan's mother made him return to Mr. Conley and tell the truth. Shan arrived at the store in time to see Mr. Conley fill the sack with flour, and the flour sift to the floor. Shan realized his dishonesty caused problems for others, and though it might have only been a penny, you couldn't put a price on honesty. Shan felt much better after telling the truth, just like I had after apologizing to my family.

With the book finished, it is now bedtime. Chloe and I are snuggled up, ready for sweet dreams. We have many places left to see in Kentucky. Next time, see if we have stopped in your town. In the meantime, obey your parents, tell the truth, and Work and Dream Like a BIG DOG!

By'n by hard times come a-knocking at the door,
Then, my Old Kentucky Home, good night!

Chapter 7

Hello, Woody Readers! Here we are on the Woody Bus traveling down the highway, singing country songs. Our favorite is Billy Ray Cyrus' "Achy Breaky Heart." Chloe has the prettiest voice. She could easily have a singing career! "Why country songs?" you ask. "Well, we are driving on the Country Music Highway!" We bid farewell to Clifford (Kentucky, that is) and headed north on Highway 23. As soon as we entered the highway, we kept seeing signs such as "Country Music Highway – The Judds" or "Country Music Highway – Patty Loveless". So many of country music's greatest singers are from Eastern KY – so many that they have their own highway! In fact, this 150 mile road represents more country singers than anywhere else in the U.S.A.! There was no need to have the radio on, Chloe and I sang every country song we knew; keeping Mommy and Daddy very entertained! When we finally finished the last verse of "Mama, He's Crazy", we saw "Welcome to Ashland!"

Ashland is a city where Kentucky, Ohio, and West Virginia come together. Ashland isn't only known for great musicians, but also for the Ashland Oil Refinery, Ashland Community College, and the Jesse Stuart Foundation. Being the Jesse Stuart fan, we had to stop and visit. We couldn't believe how many books we saw! There were thousands of books. Of course we saw Jesse Stuart's books, but there were also books by other Kentucky authors. "Do you have any books written by a wiener dog?" I asked the lady at the help desk. "Well, yes. We have the Woody, The Kentucky Wiener books here!" Chloe and I jumped for joy! We couldn't believe our books were in the Jesse Stuart Foundation. We felt proud to have our books on the shelves with so many wonderful writers like Mr. Stuart! Once again, I felt goosebumps, and my Unbridled Spirit growing!

We left Ashland and kept traveling northwest. We were careful to stay inside the boundaries of Kentucky. We had learned enough about the state to realize we didn't ever want to live anywhere else – not in New York City, not in Los Angeles, not even in sunny Florida!

Back on the road, Chloe spotted a sign that read, "Adopt a Highway". We laughed. Whoever heard of adopting a highway? We knew children who had been adopted, animals like me who had been adopted, but a highway? Mommy said that businesses or companies would choose a highway in their town to keep clean. I asked Mommy why roads got dirty. She said people threw trash on the highway and didn't pick up after themselves. Chloe and I couldn't believe that. We never threw our milk bone wrappers out the window. I decided it must be people from other states putting the trash on our highways. People with Unbridled Spirit would never do such a thing!

Seventy five miles northwest of Ashland was Maysville. Maysville reminded me of my birthplace. Like Paducah, Maysville is located on the Ohio River and also has the most beautiful murals all along the floodwall. Chloe and I still didn't see any murals of wiener dogs, but they were pretty just the same! We kept winding around the top part of our state and couldn't believe what we found in Northern KY! Northern Kentucky was a great big city all by itself! When we saw the Cincinnati Airport, I thought Dad had made a wrong turn and

NORTHERN
KENTUCKY
SHARKS

we were in Ohio. Believe it or not, the Cincinnati Airport is actually in Kentucky! It didn't start out that way however. It was originally called Lunken Airport and was located in – you guessed it – Cincinnati, but the Ohio River flood of 1937 put the airport underwater. After travelers started calling it "Sunken Lunken Airport", Cincinnati started looking for a new location. It has been in Kentucky ever since!

The river wasn't the only place we saw water. Newport Aquarium had so much water it was a fish's paradise! The aquarium holds over 1 million gallons of water! (Kentucky just loves water, doesn't it?) Over 11,000 marine animals live at the Newport Aquarium. Chloe and I were very still and quite, hoping the sharks wouldn't see us! After practicing our best "fish lips", it was time for lunch. We had a tasty fish lunch at the levee. Mom assured us the lunch was not caught at the aquarium.

I was feeling pretty tired, ready for a cat nap. I had almost closed my eyes when I saw, "Big Bone Lick State Park". If Newport Aquarium was a fish's paradise, then Big Bone had to be heaven on earth for a dog. Would it be a Milk Bone, or a rib bone? Chloe and I were excited about finding out. In fact, that is where we are now. We are stopping the bus, ready to go, licking our chops. Tune back in next week to see if we are still gnawing on a bone here, or if we have driven to see you!

Have a great week. Keep reading, listen to your parents, and Work and Dream Like a Big Dog!

Chapter 8

Kentucky Greetings, Woody Readers! Big Bone Lick State Park was not a bone for dogs, but a place where prehistoric animals went to escape the Ice Age over 12,000 years ago. We saw some big old bones, but none that a wiener dog would want. Therefore, we settled for a Milk BoneÒ, bid farewell to Northern Kentucky, and then went to discover more of the Bluegrass.

As we approached Lexington, we began seeing the prettiest horse farms. There were horses everywhere grazing in green pastures. I wondered if they were eating or trying to see if the grass was really blue. Did you know one of our most famous Kentuckians is a horse from Lexington named Man o' War. He started racing in 1919 and won 20 out of 21 races while weighing over 1100 pounds! When Man o' War died in 1947 at 30 years old, he was so popular that his funeral was broadcast nationally over the radio. He is buried in the Kentucky Horse Park. I bet Man o' War is the horse outlined on all the Unbridled Spirit signs.

We could have spent hours looking at the horses but we had other important business ahead. It was Saturday which meant "Football Time in the Bluegrass". Kick-off was hours away, which gave us time to tailgate with our fellow CAT fans. We headed to our usual tailgating spot, the corner of Cooper and Nicholasville Road to prepare for the game. I love tailgating!

LEXINGTON

After we parked we put on our blue jerseys and joined some of our friends for a game of touch football. Chloe and I weren't the greatest football players, but having four legs was a plus! At kick-off, 70,000 people were excited to see the CATS. Watching the players, the beautiful cheerleaders, and hearing the band play "My Old Kentucky Home" made me proud to be a part of the Big Blue Country.

After the game, we stopped at Rupp Arena, named for legendary basketball coach Adolph Rupp. It has been home to Wildcat basketball since 1976. It was thrilling to be standing at center court and imagine playing in front of 24,000 screaming fans. I loved looking at the championship banners hanging in the rafters. I was dreaming of how it would feel to make the winning basket when Daddy said it was time to go. I got moving fast before Dad gave me that serious "Tubby stare".

Leaving Rupp, we stopped to look at the trophies. I wondered how my favorite school had become the most winning team in college basketball history. What was our secret? An older gentleman cleaning the trophy case overheard me ask Dad this question and told us that our championship teams were not necessarily the teams with the most talent. "The teams that won it all Woody, were made up of individuals that were willing to put the team ahead of their individual stats. These players and coaches were dedicated, focused, unselfish, and willing to give their best." He also said that everyone from the star player to the last man on the bench was important to the success of the team. This sounded a lot like Dad's lessons about teamwork!

Wow! I had learned so much about champions today I didn't know whether to be happy or sad. I ask Dad whether he thought I would ever be a champion. "Woody, everyone has special gifts and talents they are born with and it would be silly to think a small dog like you should be compared to a 1,100 pound horse. But if you really want to be a champion I can sure tell you how! All you have to do is make life a little better for someone else. For a youngster, this might be a simple task like helping an older person rake leaves or spending time with a new student in your school. For an adult, a champion is someone who takes care of their family and works hard. Remember the man cleaning the trophies at Rupp Arena, Woody? It was easy to see he took pride in his job and went the extra mile to spend time with you. The only time he had probably held a trophy was to clean it, but it was easy to see he was a champion in life." Mom said some of the greatest folks in the state are our teachers, the "Champions for Children". When children and adults both strive to be champions, great things can happen in our community.

Getting back to the subject of teamwork, it is now dinner time and everyone is pitching in. Daddy is grilling chicken, Mommy is baking cookies, and Chloe is setting the table. I still need to pour the lemonade. I sure feel a lot better knowing that I am a champion, and so are you.

Lexington was sure great. Could it be the best place in Kentucky? Tune in next week to see if we are in your hometown. In the meantime, strive to be a champion and Work and Dream Like a Big Dog!

Chapter 9

Hey, Woody Readers! Well, I thought my Scooby Doo watch was cool! It can't compare to the clock I am standing in front of! This clock is so pretty, and so big! Its face is 34 feet in diameter and is made of over 20,000 plants! A fun way to tell time, and easy to see so you won't be late for curfew! The clock is probably a give-away to our location – Frankfort, our Capital City!

I had been reading about Frankfort and was eager to visit. There were so many sights to see. Our eyes got so big when we saw the Capitol building! It was enormous, and it looked like a building one would see in Paris, France. (Not that this little wiener dog had ever visited Paris, but I had read enough to know the French loved buildings like these!) It was a beautiful building with a very large dome. I just had to sniff around. I wondered if I might find a nice little French Poodle! The first place Mom and Dad took us was inside the rotunda. This was a hard word for Chloe and me, but Dad explained the rotunda was the inside area under the Capitol's dome. In the rotunda were five statues of famous Kentuckians. Can you guess who they were? Here's a clue: There was a president, a vice-president, a senator, a Civil War hero, and Kentucky's frontier surgeon. Chloe and I wanted to pay our respects to these legends by barking. When we opened our mouths, we heard the sweetest sound! We looked for the beautiful French Poodle that had to be behind us, but couldn't find her. Daddy explained there was no Poodle, and that the 190-foot ceiling of the dome made for a big echo! We asked Daddy if we could get a rotunda at our house! That was cool! Ooh la la!

While touring, we learned the Capitol we were standing in was not Kentucky's first capitol building. The "Old Capitol" as it is now called was located right down the street and was the home to Kentucky's government from 1830 to 1908. I was confused. I had read that Frankfort was named the Capital of Kentucky in 1793, just a year after Colonel Isaac Shelby was named Kentucky's first governor. Where did the government officials meet from 1793 to 1830? Mommy explained there were previous capitol buildings. When Kentucky became the 15th state in 1792, it only had nine counties. The first capitol was a log cabin and was located in Lexington. When the government was formed, there were five representatives who thought Frankfort would be a more convenient Capital because of its location on the Kentucky River. That was over 200 years ago. Now we have a beautiful Capitol building and 120 counties!

We wished we would have had more time at the Capitol. I wanted to pass the "No More Serving Hot Dogs in School Cafeterias" bill as well as make the wiener dog the official state animal, but my Scooby watch and the floral clock said it was getting late - and was time for dinner. Chloe and I begged, barked, and wagged our tails pleading with Mom and Dad to take us to the Governor's Mansion. Mommy said it was not polite to arrive at someone's house without calling, especially at dinner time, but she and Dad did agree to drive us by the mansion so we could bark and wave. Like the Capitol, the Governor's Mansion was beautiful, and had so much history. It had been the home to 23 Kentucky governors since 1914. We wondered how many puppy dogs had lived there.

FRANKFORT
KENTUCKY
UNBRIDLED
SPIRIT

While in Frankfort, Chloe and I had learned so much about Kentucky – or Kaintuckee as the pioneers once called it. In fact, before Kentucky became a state, it was part of Virginia. To think I was almost "Woody, The Virginia Wiener". Hmmm... Just didn't have the same ring to it. I was so thankful for many things – especially that I was a native of the best state in the whole U.S.! Paducah, Pikeville, Bowling Green, Maysville, just to name a few, had all been great, but was Frankfort the best place in Kentucky? I just couldn't decide. Thankfully, we had other places to visit that would hopefully help make our decision.

All of this history has made me hungry. So, here I am in the Woody Bus asking the same question I ask every night – "What's for dinner?" Don't be surprised if you see Chloe and me sniffing around in your backyard. So, stay alert, keep reading and Work and Dream Like a Big Dog!

Chapter 10

Kentucky Greetings, Woody Readers! We said goodbye to Frankfort and Bon Jour to the French Poodle I never located to head west on I-64 to Kentucky's largest city. Chloe and I were having the age-old argument on exactly how this city was pronounced. Was it Looey-ville or Luh-vul? Whatever the case, we were excited to be in the middle of the 16th largest city of the United States!

There was so much to see and do, that we didn't know where to begin. We knew seeing the entire city could take weeks, so we thought we would just hit the highlights. What better place to start than the very site of "the most exciting two minutes in sports?" In May of 1875, Churchill Downs officially opened and began its tradition as the home of the Kentucky Derby. Aristides was the first winner, with the prize money totaling $2,850. One hundred and thirty years later, the winning horse could earn close to a million dollars for its owner. Chloe and I tried to run the 1 ¼ mile track, but let's just say it was not a photo finish.

Speaking of sports, I had to see that six-story tall baseball bat on Main Street. We kept following the bat until we reached the Louisville Slugger Museum. Inside, we saw how these world famous wooden bats were made. We also visited the underground locker room and the dugout. Chloe and I tried

LOUISVILLE

to hit a fast ball, but it was too fast. Dad said it was almost impossible to hit with your eyes closed. Unlike us, there have been many Kentuckians who had excelled in athletics such as baseball great Pee Wee Reese, NASCAR champion Darrell Waltrip, and the greatest boxing legend of all, Muhammad Ali.

Olympic and heavyweight boxing champion Muhammad Ali had an interesting beginning. It all started in Louisville in 1954 when Cassius Clay (his birth name) was 12 years old and realized his bike had been stolen. Cassius found a policeman and told him that he couldn't wait to whup the person who had stolen his bike. The officer told Cassius he better learn to box first. He took that officer's advice and began training. A few weeks later, he had his first fight, and his first win! I guess you can say the rest is history. Out of all of the people in the world Ali was chosen to light the Olympic Torch in Atlanta

Before lunch, we made our way to the campus of the University of Louisville, home of the Cardinals. We toured the campus, and Freedom Hall – where the Cardinals play basketball. Chloe and I spent some time in the gym, looking at all the banners and pictures. We saw where the Cards had won two NCAA championships! With Kentucky's seven NCAA wins, that made a total of nine NCAA championships for our state! I also noticed the coach in the current photo looked like the same man in a team picture of UK. Dad just shook his head and asked where I had been all these years.

Finding a place to eat in Louisville was easy since this city has over 2,500 restaurants. We agreed on Kaelin's, who stakes a claim to being the birthplace of the cheeseburger. Chloe and I love a good, old-fashioned burger. In 1934, you could have had a cheeseburger Kaelin's for 15 cents. As you can imagine, the burgers are more than a few nickels today, but very tasty.

After lunch, we crawled back in the Woody Bus to finish

our day. Heading south on I-65, we were only 20 miles from our doghouse in Shepherdsville. We all agreed it would be a good time to bring the tour to a temporary stop and spend some much needed time at home. The longer we were away from home I realized it was going to be impossible to find the best place in Kentucky. The state was so big and each town was very unique. I enjoyed every minute of the trip but I was getting more and more confused.

After a twenty minute ride we returned home to find our brothers and sisters anxiously awaiting our arrival. They greeted us with wagging tails and sloppy kisses. I didn't realize we had missed each other so much. We spent the first hour back at home running around the lake, playing, and having fun. When I laid down to rest it suddenly hit me! After searching the state for ten weeks looking for the best place, I realized it was the place I called home. It makes me feel unbridled, happy and free.

So, here we are, in my own backyard, remembering all of the great people and places we've seen along the way. Thanks for taking the time to tag along with us. Don't be sad, this isn't the end of the tour or our tails, just a break. You never know when this little wiener dog will show up in your school or community. Remember, listen to your parents, be a champion, and Work and Dream Like A Big Dog!